# Also by Paul Fleischman

*The Birthday Tree*

*Coming-and-Going Men*

*Graven Images*

*The Half-a-Moon Inn*

*Path of the Pale Horse*

*Rear-View Mirrors*

*I Am Phoenix:*
*Poems for Two Voices*

# JOYFUL NOISE
## *Poems for Two Voices*

# JOYFUL NOISE
## *Poems for Two Voices*

### PAUL FLEISCHMAN
*illustrated by Eric Beddows*

*A Charlotte Zolotow Book*
*Harper & Row, Publishers*

*Library of Congress Cataloging-in-Publication Data*
*Fleischman, Paul.*
  *Joyful noise.*

  *"A Charlotte Zolotow book."*
  *Summary: A collection of poems describing the*
*characteristics and activities of a variety of insects.*
    *1. Insects—Juvenile poetry.    2. Children's*
*poetry, American.    [1. Insects—Poetry.    2. American*
*poetry]    I. Beddows, Eric, 1951-     ill.    II. Title.*
*PS3556.L42268J69  1988        811'.54        87-45280*
*ISBN 0-06-021852-5*
*ISBN 0-06-021853-3 (lib. bdg.)*

*Typography by Constance Fogler*
*3  4  5  6  7  8  9  10*

*For Seth, our porch light*
P. F.

*for E. H. and Echo Hill Farm with its*
*wonderful fireflies*
E. B.

# CONTENTS

## NOTE

The following poems were written to be read aloud by
two readers at once, one taking the left-hand part, the other taking
the right-hand part. The poems should be read from top to bottom,
the two parts meshing as in a musical duet. When both readers
have lines at the same horizontal level, those lines
are to be spoken simultaneously.

# JOYFUL NOISE
*Poems for Two Voices*

# Grasshoppers

Sap's rising

Grasshoppers are
hatching out
Autumn-laid eggs

Young stepping

Ground's warming

Grasshoppers are
hatching out

splitting

into spring

Grasshoppers
hopping
high
Grassjumpers
jumping

Vaulting from
leaf to leaf
stem to stem
plant to plant

leapers
Grass-
bounders

springers
Grass-
soarers
Leapfrogging
longjumping
grasshoppers.

Grasshoppers
hopping

Grassjumpers
jumping
far

leaf to leaf
stem to stem
Grass-
leapers

bounders
Grass-
springers

soarers
Leapfrogging
longjumping
grasshoppers.

# *Water Striders*

---

Whenever we're asked
if we walk upon water
we answer

To be sure.

Whenever we're asked
if we walk upon water
we answer
Of course.

It's quite true.

Whenever we're asked
if we walk on it often
we answer
Quite often.

All day through.
Should we be questioned
on whether it's easy
we answer

A snap.

Should we be told
that it's surely a miracle
we reply
Balderdash!

Nonsense!
Whenever we're asked
for instructions
we always say

and do as we do.

Whenever we're asked
if we walk on it often
we answer

Each day.

Should we be questioned
on whether it's easy
we answer
Quite easy.

It's a cinch.
Should we be told
that it's surely a miracle
we reply

Rubbish!

Whenever we're asked
for instructions
we always say
Come to the pond's edge

Put down one foot

and then put down another,

resting upon the thin film
on the surface.

Believe me, there's no call
at all to be nervous

as long as you're reasonably
mindful that you—

But by that time our student       But by that time our student
no matter how prudent
has usually                        has usually
                                   don't ask me why
sunk from view.                    sunk from view.

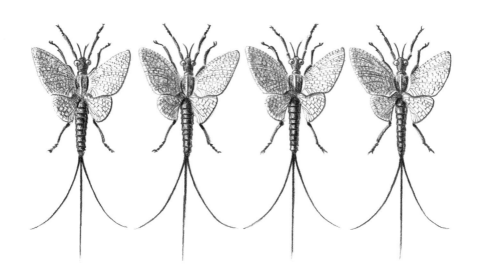

# *Mayflies*

Your moment

Your hour

Your trifling day

We're mayflies
just emerging

Mayfly month

Mayfly year

Our life
We're mayflies
just emerging

rising from the river,
born this day in May

                birthday

and dying day,

                this particle of time

this single sip of living

                all that we're allowed.

We're mayflies          We're mayflies
by the millions        by the millions
fevered

                frenzied

rushed

                no redwood's centuries
                to squander as we please.

We're mayflies          We're mayflies
swarming, swerving,    swarming, swerving,
rising high

                then falling,

courting on the wing,

                then mating in midair.

We're mayflies          We're mayflies
laying eggs             laying eggs
our final, frantic act.

Sun's low

light's weak

in haste we launch them
down the stream.

We're mayflies
lying dying
floating by the millions

We're mayflies
lying dying

on the very stream

from which we sprung
so very long ago

back when we were
young.

this morning
back when we were
young.

# *Fireflies*

Light

Night
is our parchment

Light
is the ink we use

Night

We're
fireflies

fireflies
flitting

fireflies
glimmering

glowing
Insect calligraphers
practicing penmanship

Six-legged scribblers
of vanishing messages,

flickering

flashing

fireflies
gleaming

Insect calligraphers

copying sentences
Six-legged scribblers

fleeting graffiti

Fine artists in flight
adding dabs of light

Signing the June nights
as if they were paintings

flickering
fireflies
fireflies.

Fine artists in flight

bright brush strokes
Signing the June nights
as if they were paintings
We're
fireflies
flickering
fireflies.

# *Book Lice*

---

I was born in a
fine old edition of Schiller

          While I started life
          in a private eye thriller

We're book lice         We're book lice
who dwell             who dwell
in these dusty bookshelves.    in these dusty bookshelves.
Later I lodged in
Scott's works—volume 50

          While I passed my youth
          in an Agatha Christie

We're book lice
attached
despite contrasting pasts.
One day, while in search of
a new place to eat

We're book lice
who chew
on the bookbinding glue.
We honeymooned in an
old guide book on Greece

We're book lice
attached
despite contrasting pasts.

He fell down seven shelves,
where we happened to meet
We're book lice
who chew
on the bookbinding glue.

I missed Conan Doyle,
he pined for his Keats
We're book lice
fine mates
despite different tastes.

We're book lice
fine mates
despite different tastes.
So we set up our home
inside Roget's Thesaurus

Not far from my mysteries,
close to his Horace
We're book lice
adoring
despite his loud snoring.

We're book lice
adoring
despite her loud snoring.
And there we've resided,
and there we'll remain,

He nearby his Shakespeare,
I near my Spillane
We're book-loving
book lice
plain proof of the fact

We're book-loving
book lice

which I'm certain I read
in a book some months back
that opposites
often are known
to attract.

that opposites
often are known
to attract.

# The Moth's Serenade

Porch
light,
hear my plight!
I drink your light
like nectar

by day
Gaze in your eyes
all night
Porch light!

Porch
light,
hear my plight!

like nectar
Dream of you
by day

all night
Porch light!

Bright paradise!
I am
your seeking
circling                    seeking
sighing                     circling
lovesick                    sighing
knight
You are                     You are
                            my soul's
my soul's                   desire
desire                      my prize
my prize                    my eyes'
                            delight
Porch light!                Porch light!
My shining star!

                            My compass needle's North!
"Keep back," they say       "Keep back," they say
I can't!
"Don't touch," they say     "Don't touch," they say
                            I must!
Porch light!                Porch light!
Let's clasp                 Let's kiss
Let's kiss                  Let's clasp
Let's marry for a trice!    Let's marry for a trice!

( 19 )

Porch light!

Let's meet

Let's merge

Let's live for love!

For light!

Porch light!

Let's merge

Let's meet

For light!

( 20 )

# *Water Boatmen*

"Stroke!"
We're water boatmen
"Stroke!"

"Stroke!"
We're cockswain calling
"Stroke!"

"Stroke!"

"Stroke!"

"Stroke!"
up early, rowing
"Stroke!"

"Stroke!"
and oarsmen straining
"Stroke!"

and six-man racing shell
rolled into one.

We're water boatmen
"Stroke!"                    "Stroke!"
worn-out from rowing
"Stroke!"                    "Stroke!"
                             Bound for the bottom
"Stroke!"                    "Stroke!"
of this deep millpond
"Stroke!"                    "Stroke!"
                             where we arrive
and shout the order
"Rest!"                      "Rest!"

# *The Digger Wasp*

I will never
see my children,

they will never
gaze on me.

I'll have died

when they're emerging
next July.

So it must be.                So it must be.

I'm digging now
for their protection,

far underground,
they'll recognize
my deep affection.


stung and paralyzed,

for them to eat
they'll know as well
that I was wise.


in spite of every
interference,

and thieving beetles,
they'll discern
my perseverance.

Yet, when they
behold the home


safe and snug

they'll recognize
my deep affection.
When they hatch
and find a caterpillar,

left by me

they'll know as well
that I was wise.
When they learn
I'd dragged it there


weeds and rocks

they'll discern
my perseverance.
While, cocooned,

safe from snow
and ice and chill,

and thank me for
my formidable
digging skill.

to climb up from their cells

and fly away
my young will
know me well.

never to be looked upon,

in replica
and know that they, in turn,
were cherished

whose face and form
they never saw.

they pass the winter

they'll perceive

my formidable
digging skill.
By the time they're
ready, next July,

and break the burrow's seal

my young will
know me well.
When they care
for their own children,

they'll feel my love
in replica

by the mother digger wasp
whose face and form
they never saw.

# *Cicadas*

Afternoon, mid-August
Two cicadas singing

Two cicadas singing
Air kiln-hot, lead-heavy

Five cicadas humming
Thunderheads northwestward

Five cicadas humming

Twelve cicadas buzzing

Twelve cicadas buzzing
Up and down the street

the mighty choir's
assembling

the mighty choir's
assembling

Shrill cica-
das
droning

Three years
spent underground

in darkness
Now they're breaking ground

splitting skins
and singing

rejoicing

fervent praise

their hymn
sung to the sun
Cicadas


Ci-
cadas
droning
in the elms
Three years

among the roots
in darkness

and climbing up
the tree trunks

and singing
Jubilant
cicadas
pouring out their
fervent praise
for heat and light
their hymn

Cicadas
whining

whin-
ing

        ci-
        cadas
        whirring

whir-
ring

        ci-
        cadas
        pulsing

pulsing
chanting from the treetops    chanting from the treetops
sending
forth their          sending
booming          forth their
boisterous         booming
joyful noise!        joyful noise!

# *Honeybees*

Being a bee

is a pain.

I'm a worker
I'll gladly explain.

I'm up at dawn, guarding
the hive's narrow entrance

Being a bee
is a joy.

I'm a queen

I'll gladly explain.
Upon rising, I'm fed
by my royal attendants,

I'm bathed

then I take out
the hive's morning trash

then I'm groomed.

then I put in an hour
making wax,
without two minutes' time
to sit still and relax.

The rest of my day
is quite simply set forth:

Then I might collect nectar
from the field
three miles north

I lay eggs,

or perhaps I'm on
larva detail

by the hundred.

feeding the grubs
in their cells,
wishing that *I* were still
helpless and pale.

I'm loved and I'm lauded,
I'm outranked by none.

Then I pack combs with
pollen—not my idea of fun.

When I've done
enough laying

Then, weary, I strive

I retire

to patch up any cracks
in the hive.

for the rest of the day.

Then I build some new cells,
slaving away at
enlarging this Hell,
dreading the sight
of another sunrise,
wondering why we don't
all unionize.
Truly, a bee's is the
worst
of all lives.

Truly, a bee's is the
best
of all lives.

# *Whirligig Beetles*

---

We're whirligig beetles
we're swimming in circles,
black backs by the hundred.

We're spinning and swerving
as if we were on a
mad merry-go-round.
We never get dizzy
from whirling and weaving
and wheeling and swirling.

We're whirligig beetles
we're swimming in circles,
black backs by the hundred.
We're spinning and swerving
as if we were on a
mad merry-go-round.

We never get dizzy
from whirling and weaving
and wheeling and swirling.
The same goes for turning,

The same goes for turning,
revolving and curving,
gyrating and twirling.
The crows fly directly,
but we prefer spirals,
arcs, ovals, and loops.

"As the whirligig swims"


circular
roundabout
backtracking
indirect
serpentine
tortuous
twisty,
best possible
route.

revolving and curving,
gyrating and twirling.

The crows fly directly,
but we prefer spirals,
arcs, ovals, and loops.
We're fond of the phrase
"As the whirligig swims"
meaning traveling by
the most circular
roundabout
backtracking
indirect
serpentine
tortuous
twisty and
turny,
best possible
route.

# *Requiem*

Carolina sphinx moths
Grant them rest eternal

Grant them rest eternal
Maple moths
Let light undying
Let light undying
shine upon them.
shine upon them.
Praying mantises

green darners
rest eternal
rest eternal

brown darners
light undying.
Grasshoppers
great crested

three-banded
Katydids

northern

Cave crickets
mole crickets
tree crickets
field crickets

rest eternal

light undying.
This past night
we had the fall's first
killing frost.


Black-winged damselflies

light undying.
Grasshoppers

spur-throated

Katydids
round-headed

gladiator

Cave crickets
mole crickets
tree crickets
Grant them
rest eternal
Give them
light undying.

# *House Crickets*

We don't live in meadows
crick-et                          crick-et
or in groves

                                  We're house crickets
                                  living beneath
                                  this gas stove
crick-et                          crick-et
Others may worry

crick-et
about fall

crick-et
Spring, to house crickets,
crick-et
means no more

crick-et
Summer's the season
crick-et
for pie crumbs:

crick-et
Pumpkin seeds tell us
crick-et
fall's arrived

crick-et

We're scarcely aware
of the seasons at all
crick-et

crick-et

than the time
when fresh greens
once again grace the floor
crick-et

crick-et

peach, pear, boysenberry,
quince, apricot, plum
crick-et

crick-et

while hot chocolate spills
hint that it's
winter outside.

No matter the month
we stay well fed and warm,

For while others are ruled
by the sun in the heavens,

we live in a world
of fixed Fahrenheit
crick-et

our unchanging

steadfast and stable
bright blue
pilot light.

No matter the month

unconcerned about cold fronts
and wind chill and storms.
For while others are ruled

whose varying height brings
the seasons' procession,
we live in a world

crick-et
thanks to *our* sun:

reliable

bright blue
pilot light.

# *Chrysalis Diary*

November 13:

Cold told me
to fasten my feet
to this branch,

to dangle upside down
from my perch,

to shed my skin,

to cease being a caterpillar
and I have obeyed.

and I have obeyed.

December 6:

Green,

the color of leaves and life,
has vanished!

has vanished!
The empire of leaves

lies in ruins!
I study the
brown new world around me.

lies in ruins!

I fear the future.

I hear few sounds.

Have any others of my kind
survived this cataclysm?

Swinging back and forth
in the wind,
I feel immeasurably alone.

January 4:

I can make out snow falling.

For five days and nights
it's been drifting down.

I find I never tire of
watching the flakes
in their multitudes
passing my window.

Astounding.
I enter these
wondrous events
in my chronicle

The world is now white.
Astounding.

knowing no reader
would believe me.

February 12:

Unable to see out
at all this morning.

An ice storm last night.

and branches falling.

Yet I hear boughs cracking

Hungry for sounds
in this silent world,
I cherish these,

ponder their import,

miser them away
in my memory,

and wait for more.

and wait for more.

March 28:

I wonder whether
I am the same being
who started this diary.

                  I've felt stormy inside

like the weather without.

                  My mouth is reshaping,

my legs are dissolving,

                  wings are growing

my body's not mine.      my body's not mine.
This morning,
a breeze from the south,
strangely fragrant,

                  a red-winged blackbird's
                  call in the distance,

a faint glimpse of green
in the branches.

And now I recall
that last night
I dreamt of flying.

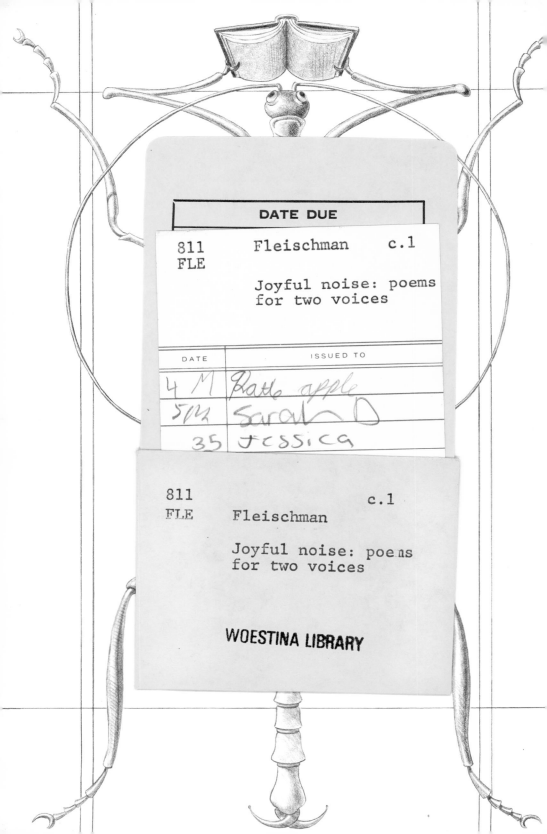